HORRID HENRY

Francesca Simon
Illustrated by Tony Ross

Orion
Children's Books

ORION CHILDREN'S BOOKS

First published in Great Britain in 1994 by Orion Children's Books
First published in paperback in 1995 by Orion Children's Books
20th birthday edition first published in Great Britain in 2014
by Orion Children's Books
This edition published in 2015 by Hodder and Stoughton

11

A CIP catalogue record for this book
is available from the British Library.

ISBN 978 1 4440 1384 9

Printed and bound in Great Britain
by Clays Ltd, St Ives plc

The paper and board used in this book are
made from wood from responsible sources.

Orion Children's Books
An imprint of
Hachette Children's Group
Part of Hodder and Stoughton
Carmelite House
50 Victoria Embankment
London EC4Y 0DZ

An Hachette UK Company
www.hachette.co.uk

www.hachettechildrens.co.uk

For Joshua and his friends —
Dominic, Eleanor, Freddie, Harry,
Joe, Robbie, and Toby,
with love

CONTENTS

1

HORRID HENRY'S PERFECT DAY

Henry was horrid.

Everyone said so, even his mother.

Henry threw food, Henry snatched, Henry pushed and shoved and pinched. Even his teddy, Mr Kill, avoided him when possible.

His parents despaired.

"What are we going to do about that horrid boy?" sighed Mum.

"How did two people as nice as us have such a horrid child?" sighed Dad.

When Horrid Henry's parents took Henry to school they walked behind him and pretended he was not theirs.

Children pointed at Henry and whispered to their parents, "That's Horrid Henry."

"He's the boy who threw my jacket in the mud."

"He's the boy who squashed Billy's beetle."

"He's the boy who . . ." Fill in whatever terrible deed you like. Horrid Henry was sure to have done it.

Horrid Henry had
a younger brother.
His name was
Perfect Peter.

Perfect Peter
always said "Please"
and "Thank you".
Perfect Peter loved
vegetables.

Perfect Peter
always used a hankie
and never, ever
picked his nose.
"Why can't you
be perfect like
Peter?" said Henry's
mum every day.

9

As usual, Henry pretended not to hear. He continued melting Peter's crayons on the radiator.

But Horrid Henry started to think.

"What if *I* were perfect?" thought Henry. "I wonder what would happen."

When Henry woke the next morning, he did not wake Peter by pouring water on Peter's head.

Peter did not scream.

This meant Henry's parents overslept and Henry and Peter were late for Cubs.

Henry was very happy.

Peter was very sad to be late for Cubs.

But because he was perfect, Peter did not whine or complain.

On the way to Cubs Henry did not squabble with Peter over who sat in front. He did not pinch Peter and he did not shove Peter.

Back home, when Perfect Peter built a castle, Henry did not knock it down. Instead, Henry sat on the sofa and read a book.

Mum and Dad ran into the room.

"It's awfully quiet in here," said Mum. "Are you being horrid, Henry?"

"No," said Henry.

"Peter, is Henry knocking your castle down?"

Peter longed to say "yes". But that would be a lie.

"No," said Peter.

He wondered why Henry was behaving so strangely.

"What are you doing, Henry?" said Dad.

"Reading a wonderful story about some super mice," said Henry.

Dad had never seen Henry read a book before. He checked to see if a comic was hidden inside.

There was no comic. Henry was actually reading a book.

"Hmmmm," said Dad.

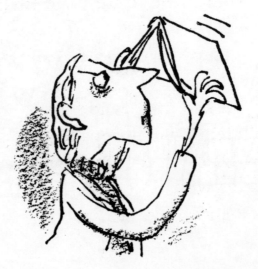

It was almost time for dinner. Henry was hungry and went into the kitchen where Dad was cooking.

But instead of shouting, "I'm starving! Where's my food?" Henry said, "Dad, you look tired. Can I help get supper ready?"

"Don't be horrid, Henry," said Dad, pouring peas into boiling water. Then he stopped.

"What did you say, Henry?" asked Dad.

"Can *I* help, Dad?" said Perfect Peter.

"I asked if you needed any help," said Henry.

"I asked first," said Peter.

"Henry will just make a mess," said Dad. "Peter, would you peel the carrots while I sit down for a moment?"

"Of course," said Perfect Peter.

Peter washed his spotless hands.

Peter put on his spotless apron.

Peter rolled up his spotless sleeves.

Peter waited for Henry to snatch the peeler.

But Henry laid the table instead.
Mum came into the kitchen.

"Smells good," she said. "Thank you, darling Peter, for laying the table. What a good boy you are."

Peter did not say anything.

"I laid the table, Mum," said Henry.

Mum stared at him.

"You?" said Mum.

"Me," said Henry.

"Why?" said Mum.

Henry smiled.

"To be helpful," he said.

"You've done something horrid, haven't you, Henry?" said Dad.

"No," said Henry. He tried to look sweet.

"I'll lay the table tomorrow," said Perfect Peter.

"Thank you, angel," said Mum.

"Dinner is ready," said Dad.

The family sat down at the table.

Dinner was spaghetti and meatballs with peas and carrots.

Henry ate his dinner with his knife and fork and spoon.

He did not throw peas at Peter and he did not slurp.

He did not chew with his mouth open and he did not slouch.

"Sit properly, Henry," said Dad.

"I am sitting properly," said Henry.

Dad looked up from his plate. He looked surprised.

"So you are," he said.

Perfect Peter could not eat. Why wasn't Henry throwing peas at him?

Peter's hand reached slowly for a pea.

When no one was looking, he flicked the pea at Henry.

"Ouch," said Henry.

"Don't be horrid, Henry," said Mum.

Henry reached for a fistful of peas. Then Henry remembered he was being perfect and stopped.

Peter smiled and waited. But no peas bopped him on the head.

Perfect Peter did not understand. Where was the foot that always kicked him under the table?

Slowly, Peter stretched out his foot and kicked Henry.

"OUCH," said Henry.

"Don't be horrid, Henry," said Dad.

"But I . . ." said Henry, then stopped.

Henry's foot wanted to kick Perfect Peter round the block. Then Henry remembered he was being perfect and continued to eat.

"You're very quiet tonight, Henry," said Dad.

"The better to enjoy my lovely dinner," said Henry.

"Henry, where are your peas and carrots?" asked Mum.

"I ate them," said Henry. "They were delicious."

Mum looked on the floor. She looked under Henry's chair. She looked under his plate.

"You ate your peas and carrots?"
said Mum slowly. She felt Henry's
forehead.

"Are you feeling all right, Henry?"

"Yeah," said Horrid Henry. "I'm
fine, thank you for asking," he added
quickly.

21

Mum and Dad looked at each other. What was going on?

Then they looked at Henry.

"Henry, come here and let me give you a big kiss," said Mum. "You are a wonderful boy. Would you like a piece of fudge cake?"

Peter interrupted.

"No cake for me, thank you," said Peter. "I would rather have more vegetables."

Henry let himself be kissed. Oh my, it was hard work being perfect.

He smiled sweetly at Peter.

"I would love some cake, thank you," said Henry.

Perfect Peter could stand it no longer. He picked up his plate and aimed at Henry.

Then Peter threw the spaghetti.

Henry ducked.

SPLAT!

Spaghetti landed on Mum's head. Tomato sauce trickled down her neck and down her new yellow fuzzy jumper.

"PETER!!!!" yelled Mum and Dad.

"YOU HORRID BOY!" yelled Mum.

"GO TO YOUR ROOM!!" yelled Dad.

Perfect Peter burst into tears and ran to his room.

Mum wiped spaghetti off her face. She looked very funny.

Henry tried not to laugh. He squeezed his lips together tightly.

But it was no use. I am sorry to say that he could not stop a laugh escaping.

"It's not funny!" shouted Dad.

"Go to your room!" shouted Mum.

But Henry didn't care.

Who would have thought being perfect would be such fun?

HORRID HENRY'S DANCE CLASS

Stomp Stomp Stomp Stomp Stomp Stomp Stomp.

Horrid Henry was practising his elephant dance.

Tap Tap Tap Tap Tap Tap Tap Tap.

Perfect Peter was practising his raindrop dance.

Peter was practising being a raindrop for his dance class show.

Henry was also supposed to be practising being a raindrop.

But Henry did not want to be a raindrop. He did not want to be a tomato, a string bean, or a banana either.

Stomp Stomp Stomp went Henry's heavy boots.

Tap Tap Tap went Peter's tap shoes.

"You're doing it wrong, Henry," said Peter.

"No I'm not," said Henry.

"You are too," said Peter. "We're supposed to be raindrops."

Stomp Stomp Stomp went Henry's boots. He was an elephant smashing his way through the jungle, trampling on everyone who stood in his way.

"I can't concentrate with you stomping," said Peter. "And I have to practise my solo."

"Who cares?" screamed Horrid Henry. "I hate dancing, I hate dance class, and most of all, I hate you!"

This was not entirely true. Horrid Henry loved dancing. Henry danced in his bedroom. Henry danced up and down the stairs. Henry danced on the new sofa and on the kitchen table.

What Henry hated was having to dance with other children.

"Couldn't I go to karate instead?" asked Henry every Saturday.

"No," said Mum. "Too violent."

"Judo?" said Henry.

"N-O spells no," said Dad.

So every Saturday morning at 9.45
a.m., Henry and Peter's father drove
them to Miss Impatience Tutu's
Dance Studio.

Miss Impatience Tutu was skinny and bony. She had long stringy grey hair. Her nose was sharp. Her elbows were pointy. Her knees were knobbly. No one had ever seen her smile.

Perhaps this was because Impatience Tutu hated teaching.

Impatience Tutu hated noise.

Impatience Tutu hated children.

But most of all Impatience Tutu hated Horrid Henry.

This was not surprising. When Miss

Tutu shouted, "Class, lift your left legs," eleven left legs lifted. One right leg sagged to the floor.

When Miss Tutu screamed, "Heel, toe, heel, toe," eleven dainty feet tapped away. One clumpy foot stomped toe, heel, toe, heel.

When Miss Tutu bellowed, "Class, skip to your right," eleven bodies turned to the right. One body galumphed to the left.

Naturally, no one wanted to dance with Henry. Or indeed, anywhere near Henry. Today's class, unfortunately, was no different.

"Miss Tutu, Henry is treading on my toes," said Jumpy Jeffrey.

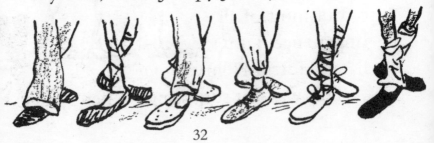

32

"Miss Tutu, Henry is kicking my legs," said Lazy Linda.

"Miss Tutu, Henry is bumping me," said Vain Violet.

"HENRY!" screeched Miss Tutu.

"Yeah," said Henry.

"I am a patient woman, and you are trying my patience to the limit," hissed Miss Tutu. "Any more bad behaviour and you will be very sorry."

"What will happen?" asked Horrid Henry eagerly.

Miss Tutu stood very tall. She took a long, bony finger and dragged it slowly across her throat.

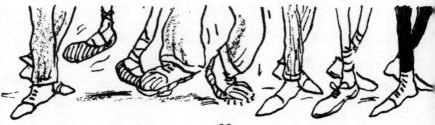

Henry decided that he would rather live to do battle another day. He stood on the side, gnashing his teeth, pretending he was an enormous crocodile about to gobble up Miss Tutu.

"This is our final rehearsal before the show," barked Miss Tutu. "Everything must be perfect."

Eleven faces stared at Miss Tutu. One face scowled at the floor.

"Tomatoes and beans to the front," ordered Miss Tutu.

"When Miss Thumper plays the music everyone will stretch out their arms to the sky, to kiss the morning hello. Raindrops, stand at the back next to the giant green leaves and wait until the beans find the magic bananas. And Henry," spat Miss Tutu, glaring. "TRY to get it right.

"Positions, everybody. Miss Thumper, the opening music please!" shouted Miss Tutu.

Miss Thumper banged away.

The tomatoes weaved in and out, twirling.

The beans pirouetted.

The bananas pointed their toes and swayed.

The raindrops pitter-patted.

All except one. Henry waved his arms frantically and raced round the room. Then he crashed into the beans.

"HENRY!" screeched Miss Tutu.

"Yeah," scowled Henry.

"Sit in the corner!"

Henry was delighted. He sat in the corner and made horrible rude faces while Peter did his raindrop solo.

Tap tap tap tap tap tap tap. Tappa tappa tappa tappa tap tap tap. Tappa tip tappa tip tappa tappa tappa tip.

"Was that perfect, Miss Tutu?" asked Peter.

Miss Tutu sighed. "Perfect, Peter, as always," she said, and the corner of her mouth trembled slightly. This was the closest Miss Tutu ever came to smiling.

Then she saw Henry slouching on

the chair. Her mouth drooped back into its normal grim position.

Miss Tutu tugged Henry off the chair. She shoved him to the very back of the stage, behind the other raindrops. Then she pushed him behind a giant green leaf.

"Stand there!" shouted Miss Tutu.

"But no one will see me here," said Henry.

"Precisely," said Miss Tutu.

It was showtime.

The curtain was about to rise.

The children stood quietly on stage.

Perfect Peter was so excited he almost bounced up and down. Naturally he controlled himself and stood still.

Horrid Henry was not very excited.

He did not want to be a raindrop.

And he certainly did not want to be a raindrop who danced behind a giant green leaf.

Miss Thumper waddled over to the piano. She banged on the keys.

The curtain went up.

Henry's mum and dad were in the audience with the other parents. As usual they sat in the back row, in case they had to make a quick getaway.

They smiled and waved at Peter, standing proudly at the front.

"Can you see Henry?" whispered Henry's mum.

Henry's dad squinted at the stage.

A tuft of red hair stuck up behind the green leaf.

"I think that's him behind the leaf," said his father doubtfully.

"I wonder why Henry is hiding," said Mum. "It's not like him to be shy."

"Hmmmm," said Dad.

"Shhh," hissed the parents beside them.

Henry watched the tomatoes and beans searching on tiptoe for the magic bananas.

I'm not staying back here, he thought, and pushed his way through the raindrops.

"Stop pushing, Henry!" hissed Lazy Linda.

Henry pushed harder, then did a few pitter-pats with the other raindrops.

Miss Tutu stretched out a bony arm and yanked Henry back behind the scenery.

Who wants to be a raindrop anyway, thought Henry. I can do what I like

hidden here.

The tomatoes weaved in and out, twirling.

The beans pirouetted.

The bananas pointed their toes and swayed.

The raindrops pitter-patted.

Henry flapped his arms and pretended he was a *pterodactyl* about to pounce on Miss Tutu.

Round and round he flew, homing in on his prey.

Perfect Peter stepped to the front and began his solo.

43

Tap Tap Tap Tap Tap Tap –
CRASH!

One giant green leaf fell on top of
the raindrops, knocking them over.

The raindrops collided with the
tomatoes.

The tomatoes smashed into the
string beans.

The string beans bumped into the
bananas.

Perfect Peter turned his head to see
what was happening and danced off
the stage into the front row.

Miss Tutu fainted.

The only person
still standing on
stage was Henry.

Stomp Stomp
Stomp Stomp
Stomp Stomp
Stomp.

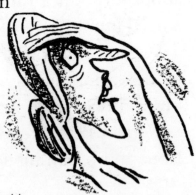

Henry did his
elephant dance.
Boom Boom
Boom Boom Boom
Boom Boom.
Henry did his
wild buffalo dance.

Peter tried to scramble back on stage.

The curtain fell.

There was a long silence, then Henry's parents clapped.

No one else did, so Henry's parents stopped.

All the other parents ran up to Miss Tutu and started shouting.

"I don't see why that horrid boy should have had such a long solo while all Linda did was lie on the floor," yelled one mother.

"My Jeffrey is a much better dancer than that boy," shouted another. "He should have done the solo."

"I didn't know you taught modern dance, Miss Tutu," said Violet's mother. "Come, Violet," she added, sweeping from the room.

"HENRY!!" screeched Miss Tutu. "Leave my dance studio at once!"

"Whoopee!" shouted Henry. He
knew that next Saturday he would be
at karate class at last.

3

HORRID HENRY
AND
MOODY MARGARET

"I'm Captain Hook!"

"No, I'm Captain Hook!"

"I'm Captain Hook," said Horrid
Henry.

"I'm Captain Hook," said Moody
Margaret.

They glared at each other.

"It's *my* hook," said Moody
Margaret.

Moody Margaret lived next door.

She did not like Horrid
Henry, and Horrid
Henry did not like
her. But when Rude
Ralph was busy, Clever
Clare had flu, and Sour
Susan was her enemy,
Margaret would jump
over the wall to play
with Henry.

"Actually, it's my turn to be Hook
now," said Perfect Peter. "I've been
the prisoner for such a long time."

"Prisoner, be quiet!" said Henry.

"Prisoner, walk the plank!" said
Margaret.

"But I've walked it fourteen times
already," said Peter. "Please can I be
Hook now?"

"No, by thunder!" said Moody
Margaret. "Now out of my way,

worm!" And she swashbuckled across
the deck, waving her hook and
clutching her sword and dagger.

Margaret had eyepatches and skulls
and crossbones and plumed hats and
cutlasses and sabres and snickersnees.

Henry had a stick.

This was why Henry played with
Margaret.

But Henry had to do terrible things
before playing with Margaret's

51

swords. Sometimes he had to sit and wait while she read a book.

Sometimes he had to play "Mums and Dads" with her. Worst of all (please don't tell anyone), sometimes he had to be the baby.

Henry never knew what Margaret would do.

When he put a spider on her arm, Margaret laughed.

When he pulled her hair, Margaret pulled his harder.

When Henry screamed, Margaret would scream louder. Or she would sing. Or pretend not to hear.

Sometimes Margaret was fun. But most of the time she was a moody old grouch.

"I won't play if I can't be Hook," said Horrid Henry.

Margaret thought for a moment.

"We can both be Captain Hook," she said.

"But we only have one hook," said Henry.

"Which I haven't played with yet," said Peter.

"BE QUIET, prisoner!" shouted Margaret. "Mr Smee, take him to jail."

"No," said Henry.

"You will get your reward, Mr Smee," said the Captain, waving her hook.

Mr Smee dragged the prisoner to the jail.

"If you're very quiet, prisoner, then you will be freed and you can be a pirate, too," said Captain Hook.

"Now give me the hook," said Mr Smee.

The Captain reluctantly handed it over.

"Now I'm Captain Hook and you're Mr Smee," shouted Henry. "I order everyone to walk the plank!"

"I'm sick of playing pirates," said Margaret. "Let's play something else."

Henry was furious. That was just like Moody Margaret.

"Well, I'm playing pirates," said
Henry.

"Well I'm not," said Margaret.
"Give me back my hook."

"No," said Henry.

Moody Margaret
opened her mouth
and screamed. Once
Margaret started
screaming she could
go on and on and
on.

Henry gave her
the hook.

Margaret smiled.

"I'm hungry,"
she said. "Got
anything good to
eat?"

Henry had three bags of crisps and
seven chocolate biscuits hidden in his

room, but he certainly wasn't going to share them with Margaret.

'You can have a radish," said Henry.

"What else?" said Margaret.

"A carrot," said Henry.

"What else?" said Margaret.

"Glop," said Henry.

"What's Glop?"

"Something special that only I can make," said Henry.

"What's in it? asked Margaret.

"That's a secret," said Henry.

"I bet it's yucky," said Margaret.

"Of course it's yucky," said Henry.

"I can make the yuckiest Glop of all," said Margaret.

"That's because you don't know anything. No one can make yuckier Glop than I can."

"I dare you to eat Glop," said Margaret.

"I double dare you back," said Henry. "Dares go first."

Margaret stood up very straight.

"All right," said Margaret. "Glop starts with snails and worms."

And she started poking under the bushes.

"Got one!" she shouted, holding up a fat snail.

"Now for some worms," said Margaret.

She got down on her hands and knees and started digging a hole.

"You can't put anything from outside into Glop," said Henry quickly. "Only stuff in the kitchen."

Margaret looked at Henry.

"I thought we were making Glop," she said.

"We are," said Henry. "My way, because it's *my* house."

Horrid Henry and Moody Margaret went into the gleaming white kitchen. Henry got out two wooden mixing spoons and a giant red bowl.

"I'll start," said Henry. He went to the cupboard and opened the doors wide.

"Porridge!" said Henry. And he poured some into the bowl.

Margaret opened the fridge and

looked inside. She grabbed a small container.

"Soggy semolina!" shouted Margaret. Into the bowl it went.

"Coleslaw!"

"Spinach!"

"Coffee!"

"Yoghurt!"

"Flour!"

"Vinegar!"

"Baked beans!"

"Mustard!"

"Peanut butter!"

"Mouldy cheese!"

"Pepper!"

"Rotten oranges!"

"And ketchup!" shouted Henry. He squirted in the ketchup until the bottle was empty.

"Now, mix!" said Margaret.

Horrid Henry and Moody Margaret grabbed hold of their spoons with both hands. Then they plunged the spoons into the Glop and began to stir.

It was hard heavy work.

Faster and faster, harder and harder they stirred.

There was Glop on the ceiling. There was Glop on the floor. There was Glop on the clock, and Glop on the door. Margaret's hair was covered in Glop. So was Henry's face.

Margaret looked into the bowl. She had never seen anything so yucky in her life.

"It's ready," she said.

Horrid Henry and Moody
Margaret carried the Glop to the
table.

Then they sat down and stared at
the sloppy, slimy, sludgy, sticky,
smelly, gooey, gluey, gummy,
greasy, gloopy Glop.

"Right," said Henry. "Who's
going to eat some first?"

There was a very
long pause.

Henry looked at
Margaret.

Margaret looked
at Henry.

"Me," said
Margaret. "I'm not
scared."

She scooped up a
large spoonful and
stuffed it in her mouth.

Then she
swallowed. Her face
went pink and
purple and green.

"How does it
taste?" said Henry.

"Good," said
Margaret, trying not
to choke.

"Have some more
then," said Henry.

"Your turn first,"
said Margaret.

Henry sat for a moment and looked at the Glop.

"My mum doesn't like me to eat between meals," said Henry.

"HENRY!" hissed Moody Margaret.

Henry took a tiny spoonful.

"More!" said Margaret.

Henry took a tiny bit more. The Glop wobbled lumpily on his spoon. It looked like . . . Henry did not want to think about what it looked like.

He closed his eyes and brought the spoon to his mouth.

"Ummm, yummm," said Henry.

"You didn't eat any," said Margaret. "That's not fair."

She scooped up some Glop and . . .

I dread to think what would have

happened next, if they had not been
interrupted.

"Can I come out now?" called a
small voice from outside. "It's my
turn to be Hook."

Horrid Henry had forgotten all
about Perfect Peter.

"OK," shouted Henry.

Peter came to the door.

"I'm hungry," he said.

"Come in, Peter," said Henry
sweetly. "Your dinner is on the
table."

4

HORRID HENRY'S HOLIDAY

Horrid Henry hated holidays.

Henry's idea of a super holiday was sitting on the sofa eating crisps and watching TV.

Unfortunately, his parents usually had other plans.

Once they took him to see some castles. But there were no castles. There were only piles of stones and broken walls.

"Never again," said Henry.

The next year he had to go to a lot of museums.

"Never again," said Mum and
Dad.

Last year they went to the seaside.

"The sun is too hot," Henry
whined.

"The water is too cold," Henry
whinged.

"The food is yucky," Henry grumbled.

"The bed is lumpy," Henry moaned.

71

This year they decided to try something different.

"We're going camping in France," said Henry's parents.

"Horray!" said Henry.

"You're happy, Henry?" said Mum. Henry had never been happy about any holiday plans before.

"Oh yes," said Henry. Finally, finally, they were doing something good.

Henry knew all about camping from Moody Margaret. Margaret had been camping with her family. They had stayed in a big tent with comfy beds, a fridge, a cooker, a loo, a shower, a heated swimming pool, a disco, and a great big giant TV with fifty-seven channels.

"Oh boy!" said Horrid Henry.

"Bonjour!" said Perfect Peter.

The great day arrived at last. Horrid Henry, Perfect Peter, Mum and Dad boarded the ferry for France.

Henry and Peter had never been on a boat before.

Henry jumped on and off the seats.

Peter did a lovely drawing.

The boat went up and down and up and down.

Henry ran back
and forth between
the aisles.

Peter pasted
stickers in his
notebook.

The boat went up
and down and up
and down.

Henry sat on a
revolving chair and
spun round.

Peter played with
his puppets.

The boat went up
and down and up
and down.

Then Henry and
Peter ate a big
greasy lunch of
sausages and chips

in the café.

The boat went up
and down, and up
and down, and up
and down.

Henry began to
feel queasy.

Peter began to
feel queasy.

Henry's face went
green.

Peter's face went
green.

"I think I'm going to be sick," said
Henry, and threw up all over Mum.

"I think I'm going to be –" said
Peter, and threw up all over Dad.

"Oh no," said Mum.

"Never mind," said Dad. "I just
know this will be our best holiday
ever."

Finally, the boat arrived in France.

After driving and driving and driving they reached the campsite.

It was even better than Henry's dreams. The tents were as big as houses. Henry heard the happy sound of TVs blaring, music playing, and children splashing and shrieking. The sun shone. The sky was blue.

"Wow, this looks great," said Henry.

But the car drove on.

"Stop!" said Henry. "You've gone too far."

"We're not staying in that awful place," said Dad.

They drove on.

"Here's our campsite,' said Dad. "A *real* campsite!"

Henry stared at the bare rocky ground under the cloudy grey sky.

There were three small tents flapping in the wind. There was a single tap. There were a few trees. There was nothing else.

"It's wonderful!" said Mum.

"It's wonderful!" said Peter.

"But where's the TV?" said Henry.

"No TV here, thank goodness," said Mum. "We've got books."

"But where are the beds?" said Henry.

"No beds here, thank goodness," said Dad. "We've got sleeping bags."

"But where's the pool?" said Henry.

"No pool," said Dad. "*We'll* swim in the river."

"Where's the toilet?" said Peter.
Dad pointed at a distant cubicle.
Three people stood waiting.

"All the way over there?" said
Peter. "I'm not complaining," he
added quickly.

Mum and Dad unpacked the car.
Henry stood and scowled.

"Who wants to help put up the
tent?" asked Mum.

"I do!" said Dad.

"I do!" said Peter.

Henry was horrified. "We have to
put up our own tent?"

"Of course," said Mum.

"I don't like it here," said Henry.

"I want to go camping in the other
place."

"That's not camping," said Dad.
"Those tents have beds in them. And
loos. And showers. And fridges. And
cookers, and TVs. Horrible." Dad
shuddered.

"Horrible," said Peter.

"And we have such a lovely snug tent here," said Mum. "Nothing modern – just wooden pegs and poles."

"Well, I want to stay there," said Henry.

"We're staying here," said Dad.

"NO!" screamed Henry.

"YES!" screamed Dad.

I am sorry to say that Henry then had the longest, loudest, noisiest, shrillest, most horrible tantrum you can imagine.

Did you think that a horrid boy like Henry would like nothing better than sleeping on hard rocky ground in a soggy sleeping bag without a pillow?

You thought wrong.

Henry liked comfy beds.

Henry liked crisp sheets.

Henry liked hot baths.

Henry liked microwave dinners, TV, and noise.

He did not like cold showers, fresh air, and quiet.

Far off in the distance the sweet sound of loud music drifted towards them.

"Aren't you glad we're not staying in that awful noisy place?" said Dad.

"Oh yes," said Mum.

"Oh yes," said Perfect Peter.

Henry pretended he was a bulldozer come to knock down tents and squash campers.

"Henry, don't barge the tent!" yelled Dad.

Henry pretended he was a hungry *Tyrannosaurus Rex*.

"OW!" shrieked Peter.

"Henry, don't be horrid!" yelled Mum.

She looked up at the dark cloudy sky.

"It's going to rain," said Mum.

"Don't worry," said Dad. "It never rains when I'm camping."

"The boys and I will go and collect some more firewood," said Mum.

"I'm not moving," said Horrid
Henry.

While Dad made a campfire, Henry
played his boom-box as loud as he
could, stomping in time to the
terrible music of the Killer Boy Rats.

"Henry, turn that noise down this
minute," said Dad.

Henry pretended not to hear.

"HENRY!" yelled Dad. "TURN
THAT DOWN!"

Henry turned the volume down the teeniest tiniest fraction.

The terrible sounds of the Killer Boy Rats continued to boom over the quiet campsite.

Campers emerged from their tents and shook their fists. Dad switched off Henry's tape player.

"Anything wrong, Dad?" asked Henry, in his sweetest voice.

"No," said Dad.

Mum and Peter returned carrying armfuls of firewood.

It started to drizzle.

"This is fun," said Mum, slapping a mosquito.

"Isn't it?" said Dad. He was heating up some tins of baked beans.

The drizzle turned into a downpour.

The wind blew.

The campfire hissed, and went out.

"Never mind," said Dad brightly. "We'll eat our baked beans cold."

Mum was snoring.

Dad was snoring.

Peter was snoring.

Henry tossed and turned. But whichever way he turned in his damp sleeping bag, he seemed to be lying on sharp, pointy stones.

Above him, mosquitoes whined.

I'll never get to sleep, he thought, kicking Peter.

How am I going to bear this for fourteen days?

Around four o'clock on Day Five the family huddled inside the cold, damp, smelly tent listening to the howling wind and the pouring rain.

"Time for a walk!" said Dad.

"Great idea!" said Mum, sneezing. "I'll get the boots."

"Great idea!" said Peter, sneezing. "I'll get the macs."

"But it's pouring outside," said Henry.

"So?" said Dad. "What better time to go for a walk?"

"I'm not coming," said Horrid Henry.

"I am," said Perfect Peter. "I don't mind the rain."

Dad poked his head outside the tent.

"The rain has stopped," he said. "I'll remake the fire."

"I'm not coming," said Henry.

"We need more firewood," said Dad. "Henry can stay here and collect some. And make sure it's dry."

Henry poked his head outside the tent. The rain had stopped, but the sky was still cloudy. The fire spat.

I won't go, thought Henry. The forest will be all muddy and wet.

He looked round to see if there was any wood closer to home.

That was when he saw the thick, dry wooden pegs holding up all the tents.

Henry looked to the left.
Henry looked to the right.
No one was around.

If I just take a few pegs from each tent, he thought, they'll never be missed.

When Mum and Dad came back they were delighted.

"What a lovely roaring fire," said Mum.

"Clever you to find some dry wood," said Dad.

The wind blew.

Henry dreamed he was floating in a cold river, floating, floating, floating.

He woke up. He shook his head. He *was* floating. The tent was filled with cold muddy water.

Then the tent collapsed on top of them.

Henry, Peter, Mum and Dad stood outside in the rain and stared at the river of water gushing through their collapsed tent.

All round them soaking wet campers were staring at their collapsed tents.

Peter sneezed.

Mum sneezed.

Dad sneezed.

Henry coughed, choked, spluttered and sneezed.

"I don't understand it," said Dad. "This tent *never* collapses."

"What are we going to do?" said Mum.

"I know," said Henry. "I've got a very good idea."

Two hours later Mum, Dad, Henry and Peter were sitting on a sofa-bed inside a tent as big as a house, eating crisps and watching TV.

The sun was shining. The sky was blue.

"Now this is what I call a holiday!" said Henry.

Francesca Simon tells you 20 things you didn't know about Horrid Henry . . .

1. **What is the worst thing Perfect Peter has ever done?**

    He once stole Mr Kill and hid him in the shower but then he felt so guilty that he put him back on Henry's bed. Unfortunately he was soaking wet, but Henry never discovered how this could have happened.

2. **Does Horrid Henry have any other clothes (apart from the blue jumper with a yellow stripe!)?**

He has five identical blue and yellow stripy jumpers because he doesn't ever like wearing anything else. He also HATES going shopping.

3. Were Henry's mum and dad ever naughty?

His mum certainly was, though she seems to have forgotten this. There's a picture of her fighting with her sister, Henry's Rich Aunt Ruby, in *Horrid Henry and the Zombie Vampire*.

They used to fight over who got the most crisps, who sat behind the driver in the car, who got the blue toothbrush, who got the cake with the most icing, and whose turn it was to choose what to watch on TV.

☆　☆　☆　☆　☆

4. **If Henry had to choose between Gorgeous Gurinder and Moody Margaret, who would he choose?**

Neither! He'd choose Miss Battle-Axe instead. Wouldn't you?

☆ ☆ ☆ ☆ ☆

5. **If Henry was invisible what is the most horrid thing he would do?**
Spy on everyone.

6. **What size shoes does Horrid Henry wear?**
Even I don't know.

7. **Has Henry ever heard Beefy Bert say anything other than "I dunno"?**
I dunno.

8. If Henry was allowed 3 wishes, what would they be?

He'd wish for all the chocolate in the world. Then he'd wish to be invisible whenever he wanted. Then he'd wish for all the wishes in the world. Henry knows bad things usually happen to people who wish for all the wishes in the world, but he's willing to take his chances.

9. Of all the things that Henry would do if he was King, what would be his very first order?

For Peter to go to prison and live on bread and water for a year.

☆ ☆ ☆ ☆ ☆

10. Apart from Fang, what pet would Henry choose if he could have any animal he wanted?

A tarantula called Jaws.

11. Have Horrid Henry and Rude Ralph ever fallen out?

You'll remember the time when Henry thought Ralph was playing a trick on him by sending love notes to Moody Margaret signed Henry and in revenge Henry wrote a terrible poem about Miss Battle-Axe and signed it Ralph.

The only other time that they have fallen out was when Henry caught Ralph red-handed nicking all the Chocolate Gooey Chewies from the Purple Hand biscuit tin –

breaking the most important Purple Hand Gang rule – the leader (Henry) always gets the best sweets.

12. Has Horrid Henry ever been to the dentist? Was he horrid?

He has been to the dentist, but he has never had a cavity, which is amazing considering how much he likes sweets. He was horrid until the dentist switched on the overhead TV.

13. Which person from history would Henry like to meet and why?

He'd like to meet any ruler whose name ends in 'The Terrible'. Especially Ivan The Terrible.

☆ ☆ ☆ ☆ ☆

14. If Horrid Henry could go on holiday anywhere in the world where would it be?

He'd like to go to his own palace and spend the day watching one of his 365 TVs, while being waited on hand and foot by Peter and Miss Battle-Axe.

15. What was Miss Battle-Axe like when she was little?

When Miss Battle-Axe was little, she looked exactly the same only smaller. She was a lot

like Moody Margaret but her secret
dream was to be a tap dancer and to
see her name in lights. Her
best friend was called Hattie
Hatchet who grew up to be
an astronaut.

16. Does anything make Horrid Henry cry?

Not really. Henry has lots of
tantrums but he screams instead of
crying. The only time in recorded
history when he cried was when Dad
burned all the chips.

17. Has Henry ever had a teacher he liked?

Unfortunately not. Henry doesn't
like anyone ever telling him what
to do. His ideal teacher would be

☆ ☆ ☆ ☆ ☆

Terminator Gladiator who would actually show him things he wants to learn.

18. If Henry could swap his mum and dad for two famous people, who would they be?

He'd swap his dad for the lead singer of the Killer Boy Rats and he'd swap his mum for the Queen.

☆ ☆ ☆ ☆ ☆

19. What is the bravest thing Henry has ever done?

There are loads of brave things Henry has done but he'd get into too much trouble if I told you. He's saving them all for his future bestselling autobiography.

☆ ☆ ☆ ☆ ☆

20. **Will Horrid Henry and Perfect Peter ever have a little brother or sister?**

Never! I don't think his parents would survive.

21. **Bonus question: Is Henry scared of anything, apart from injections?**

Yes, and the answer to this is revealed in the brand new storybook, *Horrid Henry's Krazy Ketchup*.

I'll give you a hint: It has two feet...

With thanks to all the Purple
Hand Gang for their brilliant
questions about Horrid Henry,
but a special thank you to:

Lottie	Ben
Abdullah	Anjelica
Aisha	Ella
An	Hari
Abbie	Kyle
Bethany	Toni
Joby	Isil
Charlotte	Louise
Cy	Keerthana
Rhys	Jayden
Luke	Joe

Owain Mitchell
Tom Ella
Jack Ayanle
Phoebe Toby
Charlotte Kacey
Corey Bex
Lorna Ahmar
Sammy Lewis

Visit my wicked website
www.horridhenry.co.uk
for jokes, book news,
competitions and more!

Don't forget
to sign up for my
newsletter while
you're there!

www.horridhenry.co.uk

Collect all the Horrid Henry storybooks!

☆ ☆ ☆ ☆ ☆

Horrid Henry
Early Readers

Don't Be Horrid, Henry!

Horrid Henry's Birthday Party

Horrid Henry's Holiday

Horrid Henry's Underpants

Horrid Henry Gets Rich Quick

Horrid Henry and the Football Fiend

Horrid Henry's Nits

Horrid Henry and Moody Margaret

Horrid Henry's Thank you Letter

Horrid Henry Reads a Book

Horrid Henry's Car Journey

Moody Margaret's School

☆ ☆ ☆ ☆ ☆

☆ ☆ ☆ ☆ ☆

Horrid Henry
Colour Gift Books

☆ ☆ ☆ ☆ ☆

Horrid Henry Joke Books

Horrid Henry's Joke Book

Horrid Henry's Jolly Joke Book

Horrid Henry's Mighty Joke Book

Horrid Henry's Hilariously Horrid Joke Book

Horrid henry's Purple Hand Gang Joke Book

Horrid Henry's All Time Favourite Joke Book

☆ ☆ ☆ ☆ ☆

Horrid Henry Fact Books

the orion star

CALLING ALL GROWN-UPS!
Sign up for **the orion star** newsletter to
hear about your favourite authors and exclusive
competitions, plus details of how children
can join our 'Story Stars' review panel.

Sign up at:

www.orionbooks.co.uk/orionstar

Follow us 🐦 @the_orionstar
Find us **f** facebook.com/TheOrionStar